The INVINCIBLES
The PiGLET PiCKLE

The INVinciBLES

Caryl Hart
Sarah Warburton

nosy
crow

Motorway
ool
Freddie Spoon's house
the waste lands
more flats
band stand
PLAYGROUND
RK
POSH HOUSES

For Kat xx
C. H.

To Caryl, for writing all the pictures and letting me draw them.
Thanks xx
S. W.

F

The right of Caryl Hart and Sarah Warburton to be identified
as the author and illustrator respectively of this work has been asserted
by them in accordance with the Copyright, Designs
and Patents Act 1988.

Printed and bound in Turkey by Imago

Papers used by Nosy Crow are made from wood grown in
sustainable forests.

ISBN: 978 0 85763 625 6

www.nosycrow.com

The PiGLEt PiCKLE

It wasn't really *my* fault. And you can't really go blaming Freddie Spoon, either. He was trying to be a hero. It's not as if he meant for things to get so crazy. Still, it all turned out **OK** in the end so I guess that's what matters.

Chapter One
Who am I?

My name is Nell. Nell Henry.

Actually, my full name is Antonella Henry, but nobody can say it. Or spell it. So I'm Nell. And that's that.

I haven't got a dog, or a cat, or even a mouse, because Mum has me and Lucas and the Baby to look after and can't cope with any more animals. Lucas is my big brother. He thinks he's clever because he goes to big school and has long hair and is allowed to stay up till nine o'clock. I think he is annoying because he's always looking in the mirror at his spots and never wants to play anything. Also, I've got my dad, and my granny who lives in our basement.

I live in a tall white house on a street. It has steps up to the front door. Sometimes the bell doesn't work and you have to shout really loud to be let in.

Our garden is pretty boring. It's got grass and a shed and we used to have a swing till Lucas and his friends broke it by seeing how many of them could get on it at once. They only got three, so it wasn't even worth it.

But next door is the most amazing garden you've ever seen. It's like a proper jungle. It's all tangly and Mrs Next Door hardly ever goes out there because she's in a wheelchair and she can't bend down properly to do the weeding. You'd think she'd be grumpy, stuck in a wheelchair all day, but she's not.

She's really nice. She lets me and
Freddie Spoon build dens behind the
greenhouse because she says Children
Need Wild Places. And it's true. They do.
Mrs Next Door says it's nice to hear the
sound of children's laughter.

I don't think she'd like it so much if she
knew what we were laughing about.

Chapter Two
Love Letter

So, one day after school, me and Freddie
Spoon wriggled into our den in Mrs Next
Door's garden to do some whispering. I
was feeling especially excited because I had
something really funny to show him. I dug
in my pocket and gave him a scrumpled-up
piece of paper I'd found on Lucas's floor.

"It's a love letter," I said. "Read it!"

Freddie Spoon smoothed out the paper and read it out loud.

Dear Dude

I see you walking round at school
I think you are cool
Your hair is long
it does not pong
you are sweet
so are your feet
maybe we will meet

So yeah.

from
An admirer   X

We laughed and snorted and rolled around for a while then Freddie Spoon said, "We should keep this. It might come in handy."

When I asked what for, Freddie Spoon put on an American accent and said, "You know – leverage. Collateral. Insurance."

I didn't really know what he was talking about. I said maybe we could use it to force Lucas into doing something for us when we needed him to. Then we talked about what we wanted in our packed lunches the next day for the school trip. And then Freddie Spoon said he had to go and babysit the twins while his mum sorted out his big brothers. "I wonder what they've done this time," he said.

Chapter Three
Never Eat an Egg

The next day, we went on a school trip to this really cool farm. It was the kind of place where you could feed the animals and watch eggs hatch and hide from our teacher, Miss Sweetly. It was *so* fun!

The lady gave everyone a paper bag full
of little green pellets. Freddie Spoon put
a handful in his mouth to impress Lucy
Perkins. He said they tasted of grass. Lucy
Perkins said Freddie Spoon was a loser. The
only boy she likes is my big brother, Lucas.
Eeeuw!!

First we fed the goats. I put some pellets
into my hand and the goats licked them off
with their tongues. They didn't even bite.
Freddie Spoon held his bag of food towards
a big billy goat, and the billy goat

grabbed it and ate the *whole lot* including
the bag as well!

Next we fed the chickens. Freddie Spoon
said, "Never eat an egg because it comes
out of a chicken's bottom."

I laughed so much that stuff came out of
my nose.

Then we saw the pigs.

The Farm Man told us that pigs are very clever and that some people even keep them as pets inside their house! If I had a pet pig I'd teach it to read Lucas's *Skull Man* comics and ride a bike and play the guitar.

There was a great big pink mother pig
and hundreds of tiny little piglets. I said the
teeny-weeny one was the cutest thing in the
whole world. Freddie Spoon said it didn't
matter if it was cute or not, because it was
the runt. He said runts hardly ever got
enough milk and usually died of hunger or
else the big fat mother pig rolled on top of
them and squished them flat.

I was so upset,
I shouted:

"YOU'RE
A
BIG FAT
LIAR!"

19

But Freddie Spoon just smirked. He said I could ask Miss Sweetly if I didn't believe him. I stuck my tongue out and said, "You're not my friend any more." I didn't speak to him again until it was time to go home.

Freddie Spoon was the last one on the coach. "Hey, Nelly-Belly!" he shouted.

I slid down in my seat, folded my arms and scowled. "What?" I said crossly.

Freddie Spoon plumped down beside me, grinning like an idiot. "Hey, Nelly-Belly," he said again. "I got you a present."

Now, if you know anything at all about Freddie Spoon, you will know that this isn't necessarily a good thing. The last present he gave me was a flat, dried-out toad that he'd peeled up off the road.

So I said, "Will I like it?" but Freddie Spoon didn't say anything. He just unzipped his rucksack a tiny little bit. That was when I knew we were in

Really **BIG** Trouble.

Chapter Four
Told You You'd Like It

When we got to my house, the Baby was
cleaning the floor with a piece of bread
and Mum was burning fish fingers. She
said, "How was the farm?" And I told her
about how Lucy Perkins was sick on Miss
Sweetly's foot on the way home.

Then I grabbed a bottle of milk from the
fridge and poured two glasses, and me and
Freddie Spoon rushed upstairs.

My bedroom is right at the top of our

house, which is good if you like looking out of the window at the tops of people's heads, but not so good when you have a very heavy bag and two very full glasses of milk to carry.

When we got to my room, I looked at Freddie Spoon. And he looked at me. My tummy went all stirry. My head went all hot and my arms went all goosebumpy. Freddie Spoon grinned, then slowly unzipped his bag.

"Oink!"

Out poked a little pink snout.

"Oink! Oink!"

Out poked a little pink head and a pair of enormous eyes.

"Told you you'd like it," said Freddie
Spoon. "Let's call him Kevin."

I said Kevin was a stupid name for a pig
but Freddie Spoon said he'd rescued the
piglet so it was up to him what it was called.

Chapter Five
Robbers Or Heroes?

Now, I know that if you take something
that's not yours without asking, it's stealing.
And stealing is wrong. Like that man Mum
told me about the other day. She said a
robber had been taking people's wallets
at the bus station. She said he preyed on
Vulnerable Elderly people. When I asked
what that meant, Lucas said, "It means that
the thief takes old ladies' purses 'cos they
are big and fat and can't run very fast."

I said did he mean big fat purses or big fat old ladies and Lucas said, "Both," then turned his music up and started making this groaning noise that he thinks is singing.

But what we did wasn't really *that* kind of stealing. In fact, Freddie Spoon said we had done a Really Good Thing. He said we'd saved Kevin from being squished by his mum or turned into sausages. And, oh, that little piglet was SO cute, and SO lovely and SO very, very tiny!

"Are you sure we won't get into trouble?" I said.

"'Course not!" said Freddie Spoon. "We're heroes."

I lifted Kevin Pig out of Freddie Spoon's bag and tried to give him a hug. But I don't think pigs like hugs much. He squirmed out of my arms and hid under the bed.

"Don't be scared, Kevin," I said. I held out a cup of milk and sang, "Come and drink your milky milk miiilk!"

Kevin must have been very hungry because he leaped straight at the cup and knocked it right out of my hand. Milk spilled all over the carpet. I did my best to mop it up with my dressing gown and Kevin tried to help by snuffing up the milk with his snout.

Freddie Spoon poured
his milk into my plastic
teapot and used it like
a bottle to feed Kevin.
He really liked it!

"What shall we do with him now?" I said.

"Let's give
him a bath!"
said Freddie Spoon.
"Pigs LOVE baths."

Chapter Six
Bubbles

Kevin the pig *was* a bit grubby. He smelled of farm and milk. And of whatever he had sat in when he was inside Freddie Spoon's bag. So we shooed him into the bathroom and filled the tub with warm water. I said not to make it too deep, because I didn't think pigs could swim, so Freddie Spoon poured in a bottle of bubble bath and some of Mum's special aroma-thingummy oil to make sure Kevin had something fun to play with.

But when we put him into the water, Kevin sort of panicked. It was like he'd never even had a bath before! He skidded around in the bathtub and squealed and squealed and squealed.

"Get him out! Get him out!" I shouted. "He's going to drown!"

So Freddie Spoon grabbed Kevin round the middle. But he was so slippery from all the bubbles that Freddie Spoon could not hold on. Kevin struggled and squiggled and disappeared underneath the bubbles. It was terrible. Then everything went quiet.

I looked at Freddie Spoon and he looked at me. I said, "He's dead, isn't he?" My eyes filled up with tears. I said, "We've killed Kevin in a bath full of bubbles."

Freddie Spoon put his arm round me and shook his head solemnly, like someone on one of those hospital programmes on TV. "I'm sorry, Nell," he said. "There was nothing we could do."

Suddenly, there was a loud
"Wreeeeeeep!" and a large clump of
bubbles launched itself out of the bath,
streaked across the bathroom and bolted
through the door. "Kevin!" I shouted.
"You're alive!!"

We shot out of the bathroom and crashed back into my room, slamming the door behind us. I grabbed a towel and threw it over the clump of bubbles. Then I bundled that naughty pig up and rubbed and rubbed until he was dry.

"Let's get him dressed," said Freddie Spoon.

So we found some dolls' clothes and
dressed Kevin up nice and warm. He
looked fantastic!

When Mum called us down for tea, we
put Kevin in my dressing-up box and shut
him in my room. I told him to be a good
piggy and stay put and that we'd be back
really, really soon.

Chapter Seven
Squabbling and Fighting

Dad was home from work and Granny had come up from the basement for tea.

As we sat down to eat, Lucas came in and threw down a chewed-up *Skull Man* comic, shouting what the *beep** had I done and why was *his* comic even IN my room in the first place? He waved the ragged paper in my face and shouted that it was a rare edition and that he was planning to sell it on the computer. He said I'd have to give him a thousand pounds to make up for it and that my room was a *complete pigsty*.

* he didn't actually say "*beep*", he swore, but I'm not allowed to tell you the word or I'd be swearing too.

I said what was he doing in my room anyway? Then I said, "At least my room doesn't smell of baked-beany trumps. At least my room isn't covered in crusty socks and hairy underpants!"

Then Dad banged his cup down really hard, spilling his tea and making me jump out of my skin. He said that thing about having a Hard Day At Work and why should he have to put up with Squabbling and Fighting the minute he walked in the door? No one dared to say anything for ages.

After tea, I asked if anyone wanted to come upstairs and see our new pet pig. I thought it might cheer everybody up.

Lucas gave me the evil eye and stomped off. Granny said that she remembered mucking out her father's pigs every morning before school. "I always sat by myself at school..." she added dreamily.

Dad said, "Sorry, love. I've got some drawings to finish." He's always drawing stuff, and it's all really boring. Just pipes and more pipes and bits of staircases and he never colours them in or anything. Once I added some flowers to make his pictures look a bit nicer but Dad got cross and said he'd have to start again. Grown-ups are such a mystery.

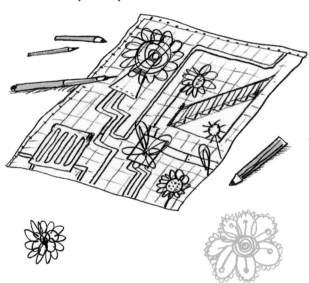

Mum said sorry but she had to bath the Baby, so we just went back to my room by ourselves.

Chapter Eight
Dollop

Kevin was standing in the middle of the room with a great big grin on his little pink face. There were clothes and books and toys everywhere. In the corner was a large brown smelly squelchy dollop.

The Farm Man *did* say pigs lived in people's houses, but he didn't say *anything* about potty training. I said, "Oh *great!*" and, "*Now* what are we going to do?"

But Freddie Spoon was killing himself

laughing. He said, "When your mum finds *that* you are going to be SO dead!"

I said, "That's a *really* big help, thank you *so* much." I was being sarcastic.

So Freddie Spoon threw my milky dressing gown over the dung heap. Then he grabbed Lucas's Pit-Stop Formula One deodorant from the bathroom and started spraying it around to hide the smell.

I tried to get him to stop but he wouldn't listen. "If Lucas finds out, he'll literally kill us!" I said. But Freddie Spoon just kept on spraying till the room was a fug of perfume.

And then the worst possible thing happened. Lucas banged on the door, shouting, "Who said you could use my Pit-Stop!"

I tried to push the door closed but Lucas just shoved me out of the way.

"What's the matter, *Nelly*?" he said. "Scared I'll catch you kissing your BOYFRIEND?"

And there was Kevin
the pig, looking straight
at Lucas and grunting
happily.

Chapter Nine
Collateral

"Get out of my room!" I rushed at Lucas, trying to force him out of my bedroom, but it was too late. The damage had already been done.

Once he'd closed his stupid gaping mouth and stopped blinking, Lucas said, "Oh, this is good! This is *really* good! You're going to be SO grounded for, like, a YEAR!"

I grabbed his sleeve to stop him going out. "Please, Lucas," I begged. "Please don't tell Mum! It's not our fault Kevin's not potty trained."

Lucas snorted with laughter. "KEVIN? You called a pig Kevin? You're even more idiotic than I thought! You have a pig called Kevin in your bedroom and you expect me to keep quiet about it?" He scratched the gross fluff on his chin and pretended to think. "This is going to be expensive. What are you going to give me to pay for my silence?"

Freddie Spoon stepped forward. "If you tell ANYBODY, I'm going to give THIS to Lucy Perkins." He waved Lucas's love note in the air, careful to keep it well out of Lucas's reach. "Everyone knows she's got a massive crush on you," he said. "She'll probably invite you round for a teddy bears' picnic in her playhouse. Wouldn't that be nice?"

Now, that's what I call a Clever Move.

Lucas was REALLY mad. "Where did you get that? Give it here! You've been in my room. You know you're not allowed. I'm telling Mum!"

Cool as a cucumber, Freddie Spoon put the note back in his pocket. "Go on then," he said.

Chapter Ten
The Plan

We all sat down on my bed and tried to decide what to do. Kevin jumped into my lap and shoved his snout under my armpit and wriggled it about. I think he was looking for food.

Lucas said we should have a bonfire and roast Kevin on a spit like they did in *Lord of the Flies*. I gave him a dead leg and told him not to be so mean.

I said maybe we *should* tell Mum. "She likes baby things. I'm sure she'll understand."

Freddie Spoon and Lucas looked at each other and shook their heads. "Lucas is right," said Freddie Spoon. "Your mum would go mad, you'd be grounded and I'd be banned from being your friend for ever."

I tipped Kevin off my lap and jumped up. "I can't believe you're siding with Lucas!" I shouted. "You're supposed to be MY friend!" But I knew he was right.

Then Lucas said, "We'll just have to take him back."

I was panicking now. "We can't take him BACK! He'll get starved or squished to death and turned into a sausage! We'll get put in prison for stealing and have to do Hard Labour and the Baby will grow up with a brother and sister in jail and we'll never be able to eat ice cream or watch cartoons ever again!" And then I started to cry. It was so embarrassing but I just couldn't stop. I can be really stupid sometimes.

Freddie Spoon said that we couldn't take
Kevin back even if we wanted to because
the farm was a
really, really
long way away
and how would
we get there

because none of us can drive?

And then Lucas did something pretty surprising. He put his arm round my shoulders and said, "Look, Nell. We have to take him back. He can't stay here. But don't worry, I'll make sure he doesn't get squished or starved or turned into a sausage, OK?"

I stopped crying then. Probably because I was so shocked that Lucas was actually being nice to me. I wiped my nose on my sleeve and said, "But how would we get him to the farm?"

Lucas grinned. "You ARE an idiot, Nell. We'll get the bus first thing in the morning."

Chapter Eleven
Escape:
Part One

Freddie Spoon was round super-early the next day. Luckily, it was Saturday so we didn't have to go to school. Lucas said if we were going on an expedition, we would need supplies. So we crept down the hall and peered round the kitchen door.

"Where's Mum and Dad?" whispered

Lucas. It was Mum's turn for a lie-in and I could hear Dad cooing to the Baby in the utility room.

"Dad's in there," I hissed. "Hurry UP!"

Lucas cut a large wedge from a big chocolate cake that Mum had made the night before. But Dad must have heard him because he called, "I'll be right there. I'm just getting the Baby out of the washing machine!"

"Quick!" I hissed. "Hide Kevin!" I scooped the piglet up, pulled my doll's blanket tightly around him, and tucked him firmly under my arm, just as Dad came through the door.

He was nuzzling the Baby's fat little
tummy and laughing. "You *are* a naughty
little squirrel," he babbled. "Fancy climbing
into the washing machine! We nearly put
you on a boil wash, didn't we?"

We smiled innocently and inched towards
the door. But Dad was looking at the cake
in Lucas's hand. "Hey, you lot!" he said.
"Wait right there!"

Freddie Spoon froze.
Lucas froze. And I
froze too. Kevin
nuzzled my armpit.

"Don't look so worried," said Dad, smiling. "Mum won't mind." He said it was good to see us playing so nicely together for a change. Then he cut three more slices of cake and gave them to Lucas. "Have one each, and there's a spare for your dolly." Dad pointed to the bundle in my arms. "Now you can have a *proper* dollies' tea party."

Well, Freddie Spoon thought THAT was hilarious. "Ickle Nelly-Welly *still* pways wiv her dollies!" he teased.

I said I most certainly did NOT! I told him that I hadn't even picked up a doll for days. Weeks, even. But Freddie Spoon AND Lucas started hopping around like frogs babbling go-goo and ga-ga, and sucking their thumbs and chanting, "Ickle Nelly Welly is a ickle baby goo goo."

I said, "You'd better shut your mouths or I'll shut them for you!"

I was SO mad.

Dad said to stop messing about and to get along now before we woke Mum up. Then he went upstairs to change the Baby's nappy. As soon as Dad had gone, Lucas grabbed Granny's shopping bag on wheels, dumped Kevin inside and we all dashed for the door.

Chapter Twelve
Escape:
Part Two

The bus station is quite a long walk from
my house. But it was so sunny and warm
and everyone was in such a good mood,
and Mum's cake was so delicious, that we
got there in almost no time at all.

When we came to cross the Busy Road,
Lucas tried to make me and Freddie Spoon
hold on to the shopping trolley like babies.
We were so busy arguing that we weren't
really paying attention and that's when it
happened.

Perhaps Kevin the pig was fed up with being bumped along the pavement? Perhaps he heard the sound of the cars and was frightened? Perhaps he needed a wee, or a breath of fresh air? I don't know. But as we were about to go through the spinny doors into the waiting room, I saw something that looked like a tiny dog run right in front of a bus and disappear!

"KEVIN!!"

I grabbed Freddie Spoon and screamed
so loud that everyone stopped what they
were doing and stared at me.

Freddie Spoon pulled me off him and ran after Kevin.

"Freddie Spoon!!" I screamed. But Freddie Spoon had disappeared too.

Lucas grabbed my hand and we ran after Kevin and Freddie Spoon. We dodged past turning buses and pushed through a queue of chattering mums with pushchairs.

Freddie Spoon was gawping at a group of posh old ladies sitting on a bench with their bags gathered around their feet.

When I tugged his sleeve he put his finger to his lips then whispered in my ear, "He's in that lady's bag."

Chapter Thirteen
Poor Defenceless
Old Lady

I stared in disbelief as one of the old ladies'
bags began to jiggle about. Then, horror
upon horrors, one of them bent down
and reached for the bag! After that, things
happened so quickly I'm still in a spin
about it now.

Just as the Old Lady reached for her bag
and I thought we were all doomed, a voice
at the other side of the bus station yelled,

"Help! Someone has stolen my purse!"

All the old ladies jumped to their feet, fussing and clucking and craning their necks to see what was happening. Suddenly I remembered what Mum had said about the robber at the bus station. THIS bus station!

I turned to tell Lucas, but he was gone! While everyone was busy trying to see the Stolen Purse Lady, Lucas had dropped to his hands and knees and was crawling between everyone's legs!

"He's going to get Kevin while nobody's looking," I whispered to Freddie Spoon.

But Kevin must have liked it inside that bag. Perhaps he was busy scoffing the Old Lady's sandwiches because when Lucas tried to get him out, Kevin let out an almighty "Wreeeeeepppppp!" and wriggled back into the bag.

And suddenly
EVERYONE
was looking at US!

81

Chapter Fourteen
Ruuuuunnnnn!

"There's the thief!" screamed the Old Lady. "HE'S GOT HIS HANDS IN MY BAG!"

She grabbed her umbrella and started battering Lucas over the head with it. Her two Ancient Companions, the Purse Lady and a tiny old man with a massive moustache, joined in.

"Get him!" they shouted.

"Call the security guard!"

"You hooligan! Fancy preying on a poor
defenceless old lady!"

Lucas didn't even think. He did what anybody would do when faced with a mob of angry old-aged pensioners. He grabbed the bag and ran.

"STOP THIEF!"

The Moustache Man launched after Lucas with surprising speed for someone so old. Freddie Spoon grabbed my hand and we hurtled after them as fast as we could.

Out of the bus station

Across the Busy Road

Past the shops

And towards the park.

Close behind us came the angry shouts of the Poor Defenceless Old Lady with the Umbrella, her two Ancient Companions, the Purse Lady and a Security Guard.

Ahead, Lucas dodged past the swings, through the little kids' tunnel that goes under the slide, and down the zip wire, closely followed by the Moustache Man. Kevin was still in the bag, squealing at the top of his little piggy lungs: "Wreeep! Wreeep! WREEEEEEEPPPP!"

And then, with the skill of a professional, the Moustache Man RUGBY TACKLED Lucas to the ground and snatched the bag. But instead of stopping the chase, the Moustache Man kept on running!

"HEY!"

"STOP!"

"KEVIIIIN!!"

Chapter Fifteen
Still Running

Lucas picked himself up and sped after
the Moustache Man. Me and Freddie
Spoon screeched to a halt, then turned and
followed Lucas. The Poor Defenceless Old
Lady with the Umbrella, her two Ancient
Companions, the Purse Lady and the
Security Guard looked confused, then set
off after us.

"He must be the REAL thief!"

"What?"

"The man with the moustache," said Lucas. "He's the real thief. He's got the bag and now he's running away! We've got to stop him!"

But as it turned out, we need not have worried. The Moustache Man was about to come to a very sticky end.

As he ran, he reached into the bag, presumably to grab the Umbrella Lady's purse. And that's when Kevin decided enough was enough. He wasn't going to stand for any more nonsense. So when a hairy hand appeared and started rummaging around in HIS bag, Kevin took decisive action.

"AAARRRGGGHHHH!"

Yelping with shock and pain, the Moustache Man stopped abruptly and flung the bag into the grass as if it was electrified!

Attached to his
hairy hand was
something small and
pink and wriggly.

"KEVIN!"

Lucas and Freddie Spoon launched themselves at the man and pinned him to the ground. I grabbed Kevin and hugged him close. The Poor Defenceless Old Lady with the Umbrella, her two Ancient Companions, the Purse Lady and the Security Guard caught up, and clustered around us, puffing and panting.

Freddie Spoon picked up the bag and gave it to the Umbrella Lady.

"My bag!" she gasped.

Lucas dug into the Moustache Man's pocket and retrieved a large purse and a pearl necklace.

"My purse!" gasped Purse Lady.

"My pearls!" gasped one of the two Ancient Companions.

"I didn't even know you'd lost them," said the other Ancient Companion. The two of them started clucking on about the pearls

and when and where they must have gone
missing.

Then the Security Guard said, "I'm
calling the police!"

Chapter Sixteen
Orange Squash and Promises

Of course, we all had to go down to the police station. Freddie Spoon thought it was cool because we got to ride in a real police car. He asked the police lady to turn on the lights and sirens but she just gave him a hard stare and carried on driving.

It took a while to explain everything, but we knew we had caught the Bus Station

Thief because there was a big picture of him on the wall. Only in the picture, he didn't have a moustache, and he wasn't an *old* man at all!

"We've been after The Swiper for months," said a jolly policeman. "As you can see, he's a master of disguises."

Then the Jolly Policeman smiled broadly, handing us plastic cups of orange squash and chocolate biscuits from a tin. "Lucky for us, you kids weren't fooled. We'd still be searching if it wasn't for your quick thinking and that smart little pig of yours."

The Old Ladies and the Security Guard nodded and smiled. They even stroked Kevin as he snuggled into my lap.

Oh, I thought. *Kevin.*

In all the confusion, I'd forgotten why we were at the bus station in the first place. We were supposed to be taking Kevin back to the farm. What were we going to tell Mum and Dad when they arrived? How would we explain why we had a small pink piglet, even if he HAD helped catch The Swiper?

But when Mum and Dad and the Baby did arrive, they hugged us all and checked we were still breathing, and listened to the whole story. And then Mum did a really strange thing. She gave the Baby to the Jolly Policeman and picked Kevin up! She tickled his little fat tummy and made some coochy-coochy-coo noises!

Then she scratched behind his ears and said, "Clever little piggy-wig," and "Fancy a little thing like you catching that nasty robber!" and "Aren't you a sweetie?"

I wasn't going to waste this chance, so I said, "Does that mean we can keep him?"

Mum handed Kevin back to me and smiled. "He IS very sweet, love, but he really belongs with his brothers and sisters at the farm."

I tried to tell her about the pigs being made into sausages, but something was stuck in my throat and my eyes were stinging, so I just sort of said, "Huuuuuuu."

Mum crouched down and put her arms around me. "Don't worry, love," she said. "I won't let anyone hurt him."

Chapter Seventeen
Robbers and Heroes

When we arrived at the farm, Dad
explained everything to the Farm Man. But
instead of being cross, the Farm Man burst
out laughing! He actually did!

He said he was very pleased to see his
little piglet again and that he liked the
name Kevin. He said that Kevin was a true
hero. He said that Kevin and his brothers
and sisters were PETS and that they would

NEVER be turned into sausages, or even bacon.

And then he did a really, really kind thing. He gave us each a special ticket that meant we could go back to the farm as many times as we liked, for FREE!

I gave Kevin a last hug and whispered into his ear, "I love you, Kevin. Don't forget me."

Kevin snuffled my face and licked my nose. I think that meant he loved me too, but you never can tell with piglets.

Then I put him back into his pen. Kevin ran straight over to the big mother pig and started to drink some milk.

The mother pig grunted happily and the other piglets all piled in too so that Kevin was soon completely buried under a heap of wriggling piglets.

It looked nice and I suddenly felt like
perhaps he *was* in the right place after all.

In the car on the way home, Lucas said, "You can give it back now, Freddie."

Freddie Spoon pretended to look confused. "Give what back?" he said.

Lucas went bright red and growled, "My note, you idiot. Give it back. Now!"

Freddie Spoon patted his pockets then said in a really loud voice, "Oh yes, your LOVE note. Of course. Here it is."

Lucas grabbed the note, stuffed it into his pocket and slumped down in his seat. Freddie Spoon grinned cheekily at me and started humming to himself.